Pat-a-Cake

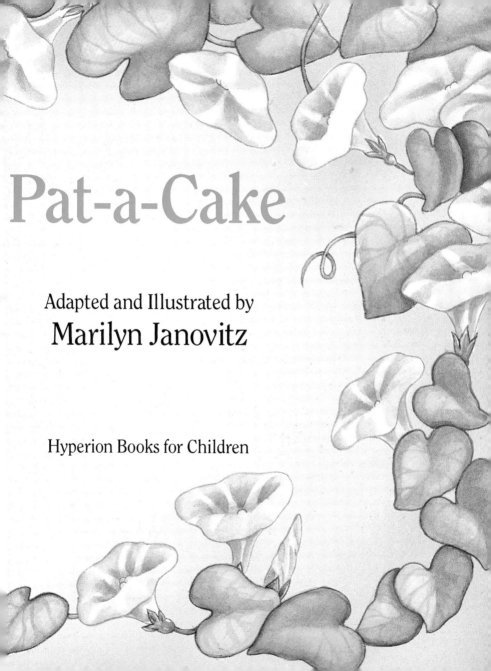

Pat-a-Cake

Adapted and Illustrated by
Marilyn Janovitz

Hyperion Books for Children

For Douglas

For information address
Hyperion Books for Children
114 Fifth Avenue
New York, New York 10011

First Edition
1 3 5 7 9 10 8 6 4 2

Library of Congress Cataloging-in-Publication Data
Janovitz, Marilyn.
Pat-a-cake / adapted and illustrated by Marilyn Janovitz.
p. cm.
Summary: This edition of the traditional nursery rhyme
features illustrations of animal characters.
ISBN 1-56282-170-9 (trade) — ISBN 1-56282-171-7 (lib. bdg.)
1. Nursery rhymes.   2. Children's poetry.   [1. Nursery rhymes.]
I. Title.
PZ8.3.J263Pat 1992 0398.8 — dc20 91-26950 CIP AC

The artwork for each picture consists of watercolor and colored pencil
and is prepared on Arches watercolor paper.
This book is set in 24-point ITC Clearface.

Pat-a-cake

at-a-cake,

baker

nan.

Bake me a cak

s fast as you can.

Pat it and shape i

nd mark it with a *B*,

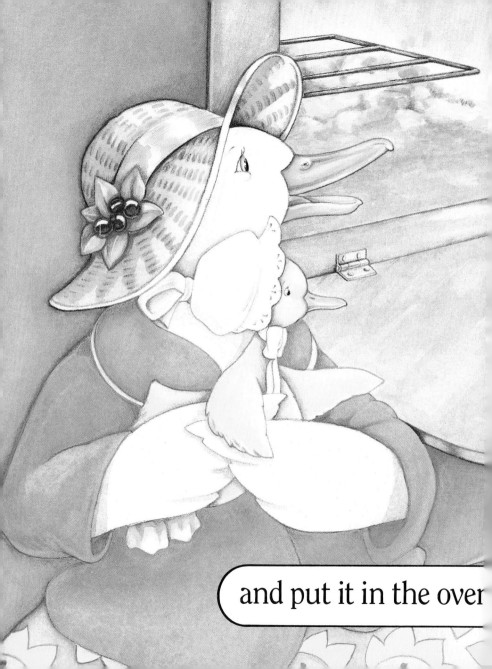

and put it in the over

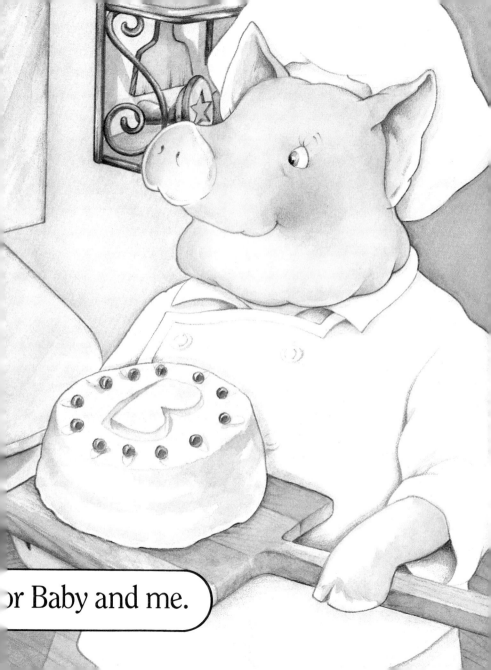

or Baby and me.

Pat-a-cake, pat-a-cake, Ba-ker's man.

Bake me a cake __ as fast as you can.

Pat it and shape it and mark it with a B, And

put it in the o-ven for Ba-by and me.